LEARNS ABOUT TRAFFIC

by Jill Kingdon

ILLUSTRATIONS BY
ERIC EISER

Delair

Manufactured in the United States of America and published simultaneously in Canada. ISBN: 0-8326-2625-2.

Dizzy heard his mother calling. "Wake up, Dizzy! Wake Up! Today is the day we're going to visit your dad's office in the city."

In no time, Dizzy was downstairs eating his breakfast of skunk cabbage and pine cones. He was very excited about going to Swamp City.

After breakfast, they set out for the bus stop. As they walked along, Dizzy looked at the houses, and the birds, and the trees.

He was so busy looking all around, Dizzy forgot to watch where he was going. WHAP! He ran right into the Fossil family's garbage cans. Garbage flew in every direction.

As Mrs. Dinosaur began cleaning up the mess she said, "Son, you must always watch where you're going—you could be hurt."

Dizzy tried very hard to remember what his mom had said. When they got to the next corner, he was thinking so hard about watching where he was going, he stepped off the curb without looking both ways.

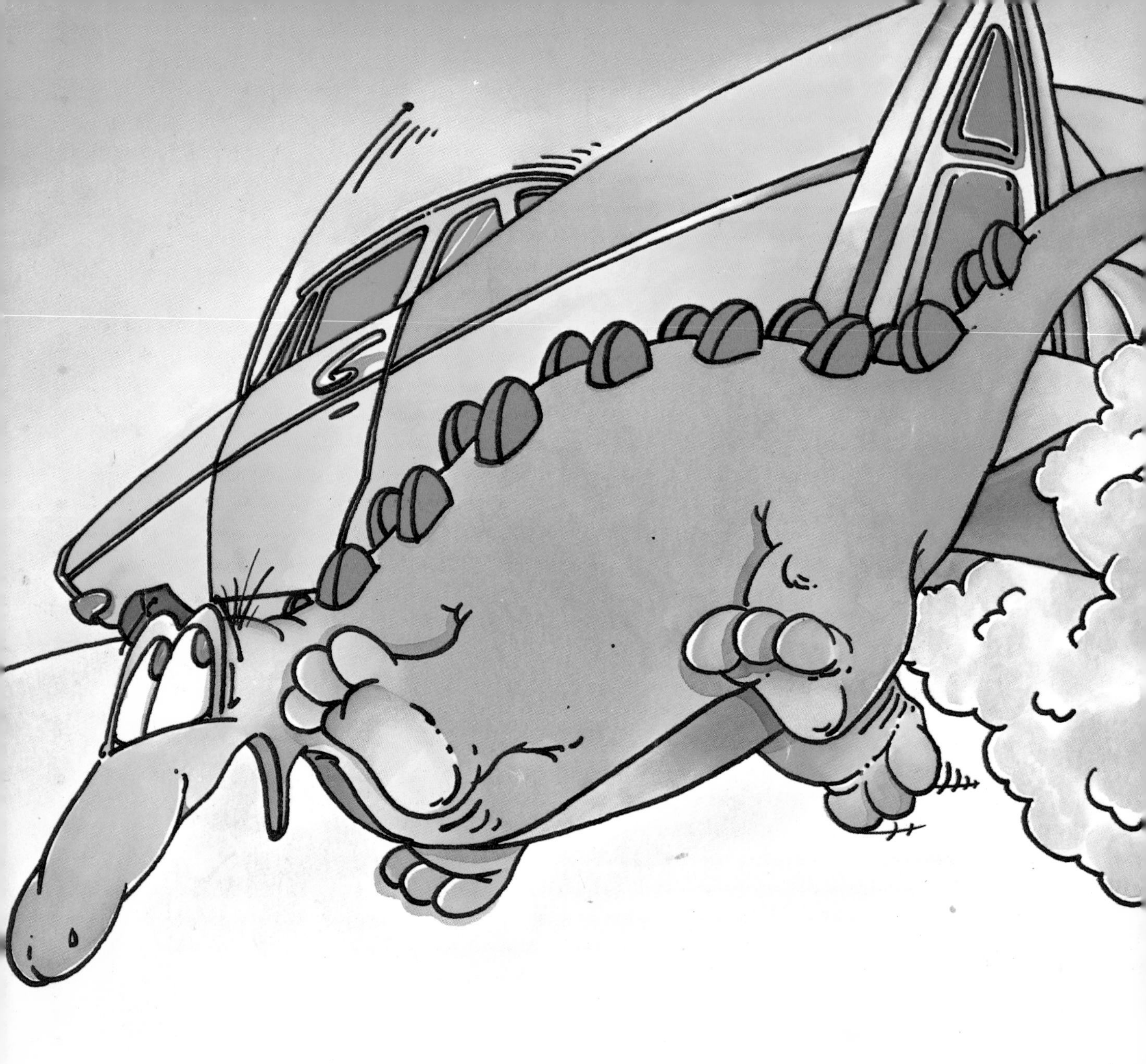

Honk, honk. Beep, beep. Dizzy was frightened by all the horns and screeching tires and angry drivers. He began crying.

"Oh Dizzy. Don't you remember? You always must look both ways when you cross the street. Sometimes cars are going too fast and can't stop."

Very carefully they made their way to the bus stop.

Once they were seated and whizzing along, Dizzy forgot all about bumping into garbage cans and stepping off curbs. As they drew closer and closer to the city, he looked out the window at all the new sights.

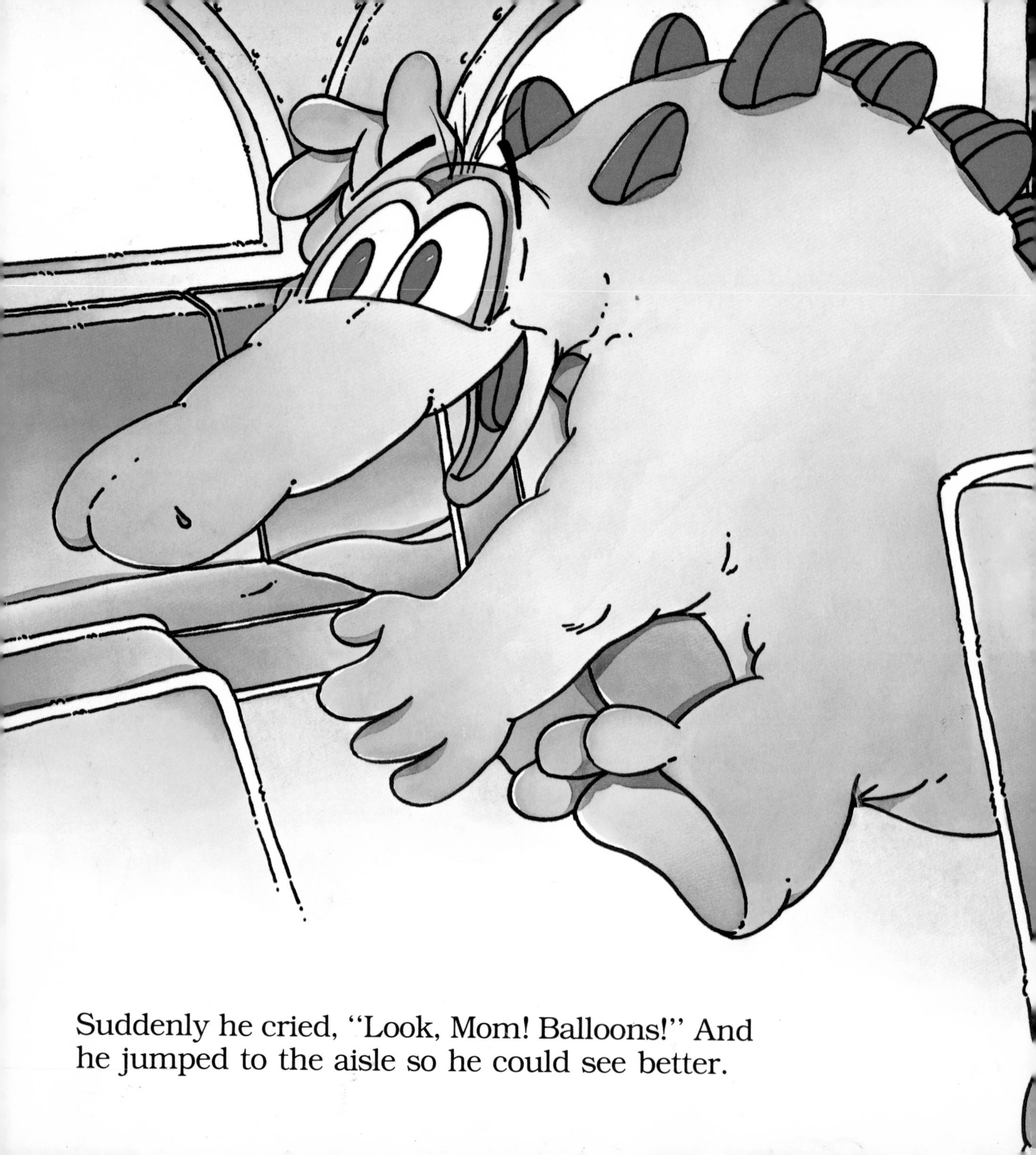

Suddenly he cried, "Look, Mom! Balloons!" And he jumped to the aisle so he could see better.

At just that moment, the driver had to stop short for a red light. Dizzy went flying!

Mrs. Dinosaur came rushing forward. "Oh Dizzy. Are you all right?"

The bus driver said, "Next time you're on a bus, stay in your seat. You could get hurt."

"Here's our stop," said Dizzy's mom with relief. And off they hopped. "Thank you," she called as the bus pulled away.

And then she turned to Dizzy. "In the city, there are traffic lights at each corner. When you come to one, remember: 'Walk on the green and not in between.' "

When they got to the next corner, Dizzy thought, "Hmmm. Was the rule 'Cross on the red cause that's what Mom said?' "

“No. Was it ‘Cross on the yellow and be a good fellow?’ No. I know! ‘Cross on the green and not in between!’ ”

“Right!” said his mother. And across they walked.

At Dr. Dinosaur's office, Dizzy told his father the new rule he remembered. "Dizzy," his mother said, "we learned three other rules, too. Can you remember them?" But no matter how hard he tried, he could only think of the rule that rhymed.

That gave Dizzy's dad an idea....

Later on, Dizzy, his mother and his father walked down Fern Street on their way to McDinosaur's for lunch. As they passed a game room, Dizzy stared inside.

WHAP! He ran straight into a hot chestnut cart. Hot chestnuts rolled everywhere. Everyone passing by began slipping and sliding and falling down.

As Dr. Dinosaur picked Dizzy up, he said, "You must remember: 'Watch where you're walking— and please! No gawking!' "

"Yes," said the lady on roller skates, "watch where you're walking and please no gawking!"

And because the rule rhymed, Dizzy remembered it.

Going home on the bus that afternoon, Dizzy's father said, "Here's another rhyming rule, Dizzy. 'Sit on your seat; don't stand on your feet.' " And Dizzy did just that all the way to their stop.

As the Dinosaurs walked to their house, they had to cross many streets. When they reached the first corner, Dizzy's mom said, "Look to your left, look to your right—any speeding cars in sight?"

At the next corner, and the corner after that, and at all the corners, Dizzy remembered the rhyme and crossed safely.

Dr. and Mrs. Dinosaur were very proud of him. Remembering things had never been easy for Dizzy, and they were glad he'd found a good way not to forget.

The next day at school, Dizzy told his classmates all about his day in the city and about the new traffic rules he'd learned.

His teacher liked the rhymes so much, she wrote them on the blackboard and had the whole class say them.

Dizzy Dinosaur is a stegosaurus (you pronounce it: steg-o-SAWR-us). The stegosaurus was a plant-eating dinosaur which was very long and heavier than a car. But its head was quite small and its brain was the size of a walnut. (Maybe that's why Dizzy is so dizzy!) Any enemy who tried to bite the stegosaurus got a very unpleasant surprise: The stegosaurus had two rows of bony triangles going down his backbone and each triangle was as tall as a three-year-old child!